2.0

D1313859

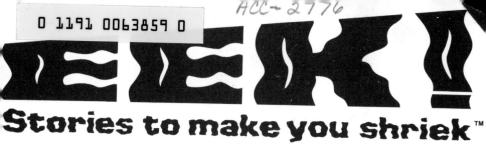

EEEK!

Stories to make you shriek™

For Beginning Readers
Ages 6-8

This series of spooky stories has been created especially for beginning readers—children in first and second grades who are developing their reading skills.

How do these books help children learn to read?

- Kids love creepy stories and these stories are true page-turners (but never too scary).
- The sentences are short.
- The words are simple and repeated often in the story.
- The type is large with lots of room between words and lines.
- Full-color pictures on every page act as visual "clues" to help children figure out the words on the page.

Once children have read one story, they'll be asking for more!

Library of Congress Cataloging-in-Publication Data

O'Connor, Jane.
    The bad-luck penny / by Jane O'Connor ; illustrated by Horatio Elena.
      p.   cm. — (Eek! Stories to make you shriek)
    Summary: A boy finds a shiny penny that he thinks will bring him good luck, but it grants his wishes in undesirable ways.
      [1. Wishes—Fiction.   2. Magic—Fiction.]   I. Elena, Horatio, ill.   II. Title.
    III. Series.
    PZ7.O222Bad   1996
    [Fic]—dc20   95-18326
                                                                              CIP
                                                                              AC
ISBN 0-448-41254-3   A B C D E F G H I J

EEK!

stories to make you shriek™

The Bad-Luck Penny

By Jane O'Connor

Illustrated by Horatio Elena

Grosset & Dunlap • New York

There it was on the ground—

a penny.

The penny was so shiny.

It made me blink.

"Ooh, look! A good-luck penny,"

I said to my pal Ben.

"Do you believe in that stuff?"

Ben asked.

I bent down and picked it up.

"Well . . . sort of," I said.

The penny was so shiny.

I had to squint.

And it felt warm—almost hot—

in my hand.

Like it really had magic in it.

"You will see," I told Ben.

"This penny is going

to bring me good luck."

The very next morning

I got to try out my penny.

My big brother Hal and I

were walking to school.

On the way I spotted

a girl in Hal's class.

"Isn't that Jenny?" I asked.

Hal's friends tease him.

They say he has fallen

head over heels for Jenny.

That means he likes her.

Too bad, because

she doesn't like him back.

The girl was closer now.

"It is Jenny!" I said.

"Will you be quiet?" Hal said.

"Sorry!" I said.

I always say the wrong thing
to Hal.

Then I got an idea.

Maybe I could help Hal.

Maybe I could get Jenny

to like him back.

I took out my good-luck penny.

I rubbed it hard.

"Please make Jenny fall

head over heels for Hal,"

I said to myself.

11

Then something strange happened.

Just as Jenny passed us,

Hal stuck out his foot.

Now, why did he do that?

Jenny went flying.

She was not hurt.

But she was mad.

"You tripped me!

Why did you do that?"

Jenny shouted.

Hal looked like he was in shock.

"Hal, you are nothing but

a big, fat jerk!" Jenny said.

And off she stomped.

"Hal, why <u>did</u> you do that?" I asked.

"I didn't mean to!" Hal said.

"But you stuck out your—"

I started to say.

"JUST BE QUIET!" Hal said.

He walked ahead of me

the rest of the way to school.

So much for my good-luck penny!

That night at dinner

my brother told my parents

what had happened.

"My foot just shot out.

It was like it had a life of its own!

Then Jenny was in the air.

She almost went head over heels!"

I was eating a burger.

All of a sudden I stopped chewing.

Hal said that Jenny went

head over heels.

That was what I had wished for!

Maybe the penny had worked.

Maybe it just got mixed up.

After dinner I went to my room.

I took the penny from my pocket.

It looked different now—

not so new and shiny.

And it didn't feel warm anymore.

What was going on?

Did it have magic in it?

Did it?

The more I thought about it,

the more I was sure.

That penny was magic.

And I had to be careful

how I said my wishes.

19

On Friday in the lunchroom,

we were sitting around

trading cards.

"This is my coolest one.

Hardly anyone has it,"

Ben said proudly.

BOTETOURT COUNTY
P.O. BOX 129

He passed around a card

of Doctor Dread.

I got to hold it.

But only for a second.

Ben was scared it would get bent.

It <u>was</u> a cool card.

"I wish I had a Doctor Dread card,"

I said to myself.

Then I remembered my penny.

I dug down in my pocket

and rubbed it hard for luck.

At the end of school,

we got ready to go home.

All of a sudden,

Ben started shouting.

"My card! My Doctor Dread card!

It's not in my desk.

It's gone!"

I helped Ben look for the card.

But it was not in his book bag.

And it was not in the lunchroom.

Ben was very upset.

We walked home together.

I tried to cheer Ben up.

"Want a stick of gum?" I asked.

Ben shrugged. "Maybe."

I dug in my pocket

and took out a pack of gum.

As I did,

something else fell out.

Ben and I stared at it.

It was the Doctor Dread card!

"You! You took my card!"

Ben shouted.

"I don't know how it got there!"

I said.

"I thought we were friends,"

Ben said.

"Well, if you want it so bad,

keep it!"

Ben shoved the card in my pocket.

Then he ran down the street.

I walked home by myself.

I felt almost sick.

How did the card

get in my pocket?

What was going on here?

Back at my house,

I sat down on a chair.

It gave me the creeps to know

the card was in my pocket.

I dug down.

I felt it . . .

and the penny.

My throat went all dry.

I remembered how

I had wished for

a Doctor Dread card.

Well, now I had one!

Was it because of the penny?

The penny looked

about a hundred years old now.

And it felt so cold,

it stung my fingers.

Yes. The penny made

wishes come true.

But not the way you wanted.

I was scared.

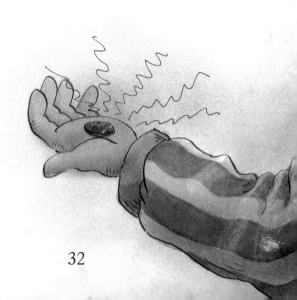

I didn't want any more bad luck.

I had to be very careful

not to make any more wishes.

Right then my parents came home.

Mom saw my face

and asked what was wrong.

But all I said was,

"Ben and I are in a fight."

Mom gave me a hug.

"We just got tickets

for a baseball game tonight.

That should cheer you up!"

I tried to smile.

I love baseball.

And it was a good game.

But it was hard to keep

my mind on it.

I bet Ben was telling everybody

I was a thief!

All of a sudden Dad was poking me.

"Look! The ball is coming our way!"

I looked up.

It was a home run!

And the ball was coming right at us.

For a second,

I forgot all about my bad day

and my bad-luck penny.

I jumped up from my seat.

I have never caught a ball

at a ball game.

Now was my chance.

"Let me have it!

Let me have it!" I wished.

The words were out of my mouth

before I could stop them.

Oh, no!

I made a wish!

I was not rubbing my penny

so maybe—

WHACK!

Something came at me

like a rocket.

Then everything went black.

The next thing I knew

I was lying in bed.

"Don't try to move now.

Just rest," Dad said.

"You are in the hospital.

That baseball knocked you out.

But the doctor says

you will be fine."

Hospital!

Now it all came back to me!

It was that penny again.

I had to get rid of it.

Who knew what would happen next?

As soon as my family left,

I got out of bed.

I felt dizzy and weak.

My pants were in the closet.

I dug down in the pocket.

I could tell the penny was in there.

The whole pocket was freezing cold!

I went to the window

and opened it.

I threw that pitch-black penny

as far as I could.

The penny sailed through the air.

It seemed to get

all shiny again!

I do not know where it landed.

I hope it is in some bushes

so no one will find it.

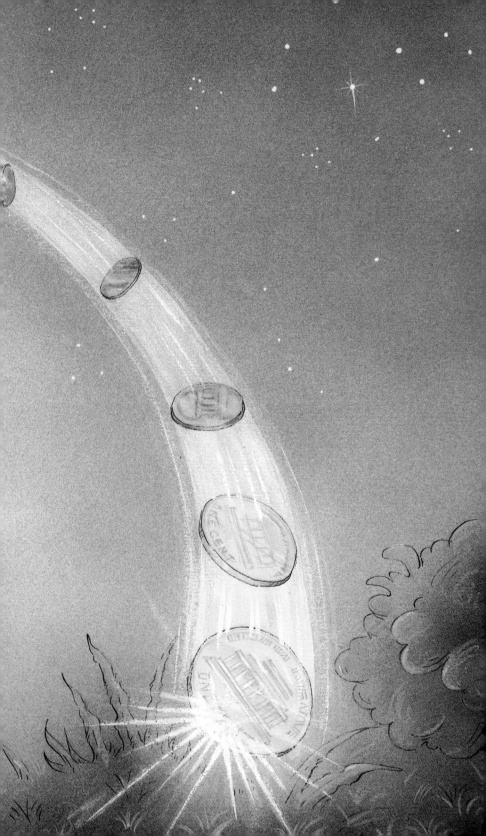

But if you come across a penny—

a penny so shiny it makes you blink—

here is my advice:

DON'T PICK IT UP!